Just like Jasper!

Nick Butterworth and Mick Inkpen

Hodder and Stoughton

London Sydney Auckland Toronto

Jasper is going to the toyshop with his birthday money.

What will he buy?

Will he choose a ball?

Or perhaps a clockwork mouse?

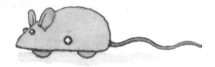

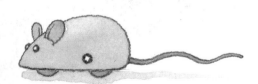

A noisy drum?

Or some bubbles?

Would he like a car?

Or maybe a doll?

Or a robot?

Will he choose a Jack-in-a-box?

No. Jasper doesn't want any of these.

What has he chosen?

It's a little cat.
Just like Jasper!

British Library Cataloguing in Publication Data

Butterworth, Nick
Just like Jasper!
I. Title   II. Inkpen, Mick
823´.914[J]

ISBN 0-340-49643-6

First published 1989

Published by Hodder and Stoughton Children's Books,
a division of Hodder and Stoughton Ltd,
Mill Road, Dunton Green, Sevenoaks, Kent TN13 2YJ

Printed in Italy